DATE DUE

D0959776

SEP 2 3 1998

OCT 0 9 1998

NOV 1 4 2001

set

Library Store #47-0119 Peel Off Pressure Sensitive

A ROOKIE READER®

MESSY BESSEY'S CLOSET

By Patricia and Fredrick McKissack

Illustrations by Rick Hackney

Prepared under the direction of Robert Hillerich, Ph.D.

 CHILDRENS PRESS®

CHICAGO

SISKIYOU CO. SUPT. SCHOOLS
LIBRARY
609 S. GOLD ST.
YREKA, CA 96097

LIBRARY OF CONGRESS
Library of Congress Cataloging-in-Publication Data

McKissack, Pat, 1944-
  Messy Bessey's closet / by Patricia and Fredrick
McKissack ; illustrated by Rick Hackney.
    p. cm. — (A Rookie reader)
  Summary: Messy Bessey learns a lesson about
sharing when she cleans out her closet.
  ISBN 0-516-02091-9
  [1. Cleanliness—Fiction. 2. Orderliness—Fiction.
3. Sharing—Fiction. 4. Stories in rhyme.] I. McKissack,
Fredrick. II. Hackney, Rick, ill. III. Title. IV. Series.
PZ8.3.M4598Me   1989
[E]—dc20   89-34667
                                                    CIP
                                                    AC

Copyright © 1989 by Childrens Press®, Inc.
All rights reserved. Published simultaneously in Canada.
Printed in the United States of America.
1 2 3 4 5 6 7 8 9 10 R 98 97 96 95 94 93 92 91 90 89

Look, Messy Bessey! What do you see?
Your closet, Bessey, is so messy!

3

See. Open the closet door,
and everything falls on the floor.

Come on now, Messy Bessey.
There is work to do.

Your room is clean and beautiful.
Now clean your closet, too.

So Bessey cleaned her closet.
It didn't take too long.

Everything looked wonderful.
But something else was wrong.

13

Messy Bessey looked around.
She really was confused.
What to do with all the
things that she never used?

A ball,
a rope,
an old straw hat,

puzzles,
games,
and a baseball bat.

17

A Halloween mask,
and a vampire cape,

dinosaur posters,
and a funny ape.

Then Messy Bessey thought of a way.
And that is what she did all day—

loving,
sharing,

23

learning,
caring,

giving it all away.

Now, look what you've done, Miss Bessey!
We're all so proud of you.

Your room and your *closet*
(just like you)

are beautiful through and through!

WORD LIST

a	didn't
all	dinosaur
an	do
and	done
ape	door
are	else
around	everything
away	falls
ball	floor
baseball	funny
bat	games
beautiful	giving
Bessey	Halloween
but	hat
cape	her
caring	is
clean	it
cleaned	just
closet	learning
come	like
confused	long
day	look
did	looked

loving
mask
Messy
Miss
never
now
of
old
on
open
posters
proud
puzzles
really
room
rope
see
sharing
she
so
something
straw
take

that
the
then
there
things
thought
through
to
too
up
used
vampire
was
way
we're
what
with
wonderful
work
wrong
you
you've
your

About the Authors

Patricia and **Fredrick McKissack** are free-lance writers, editors, and teachers of writing. They are the owners of All-Writing Services, located in Clayton, Missouri. Since 1975, the McKissacks have published numerous magazine articles and stories for juvenile and adult readers. They also have conducted educational and editorial workshops throughout the country. *Messy Bessey's Closet* is a sequel to the Rookie Reader *Messy Bessey*, also by the McKissacks. The McKissacks and their three teenage sons live in a large remodeled inner-city home in St. Louis.

About the Artist

Richard Hackney is a San Francisco illustrator and writer who graduated from Art Center School in Los Angeles, California. He has worked at Disney Studios, drawn a syndicated comic strip, and has been an art director in advertising. He has also done some acting, written children's stories, and currently is doing a lot of educational illustration. Richard also illustrated *Messy Bessey* by the McKissacks.

Richard lives with his wife, Elizabeth, and a black cat in a home on the edge of San Francisco Bay.

21537